First published in the United States of America in 2020 by Chronicle Books LLC.

Originally published in Catalan in 2018 under the title *Enigmes: Desafia la teva ment amb 25 misteris de la història* by Zahorí Books in Barcelona, Spain.

Text copyright © 2018 by Ana Gallo.

Illustrations copyright © 2018 by Victor Escandell.

Translation copyright © 2020 by Chronicle Books LLC.

Library of Congress Cataloging-in-Publication Data available.

ISBN 978-1-4521-8007-6

Manufactured in China.

Original Zahorí Books edition design by Victor Escandell and Rebeka Elizegi.

Chronicle Books edition design by Riza Cruz and Lydia Ortiz.

English translation by Feather Flores.

Typeset in Diamond Girl, Frente, Interstate, and Noteworthy.

10 9 8 7 6 5 4 3 2 1

Chronicle Books LLC
680 Second Street
San Francisco, California 94107

Chronicle Books—we see things differently.
Become part of our community at www.chroniclekids.com.

"Thank you Malena, Nico, Biel, Julia, Benat, and Naroa for always inspiring us, and for giving us ideas as fun as the ones in this book."
Victor + Rebeka

SLEUTH & SOLVE HISTORY

20+ MIND-TWISTING MYSTERIES

by Victor Escandell

Adaptation of mysteries by Ana Gallo

chronicle books · san francisco

WELCOME TO
SLEUTH & SOLVE HISTORY

History is full of real-life mysteries, but the ones you'll find in this book are all fictional. Although they're inspired by historical facts and, at times, real people, the actual scenarios never really happened.

These stories are historical fiction, allowing you to visit other (real) time periods all while exercising your logic and your imagination. These two modes of thought have served humanity well over the centuries. And now they'll enable you to travel to faraway places and historical eras.

HOW DO YOU SOLVE THESE MYSTERIES?

At the beginning of each puzzle, you will find an icon that indicates the way to solve it: with logic or with imagination.

 LOGIC    IMAGINATION

 USING LOGIC...

When you see the Logic icon, you know that the puzzle will present a setting and a clue.

• Read the whole case thoroughly and observe the illustrations carefully.

• Don't just offer the first solution that comes to mind. If you think you know the answer, check it by recreating the whole story with your solution in mind.

• Then ask yourself, *Do all of the elements make sense?*

> The solution lies in the text or in the illustrations. Read and observe carefully!

USING IMAGINATION...

When you see the Imagination icon:

• These mysteries pose unusual situations and have surprising answers.

• Remember that although these mysteries appear to be simple, the logical answer is usually not the right one. You must use your imagination to solve them.

• Think outside the box. Approach the problem in a different way.

THE POINTS SYSTEM

The mysteries in this book are classified by difficulty level ranging from 1 to 6.
The levels are featured at the top of each page with stars.

1 = Very Easy		6 = Very Difficult
★ ★ ★ ★ ★ ★	Each difficulty level has a different point value.	★ ★ ★ ★ ★ ★

LEVEL		POINTS
★ ★ ★ ★ ★ ★		10
★ ★ ★ ★ ★ ★		20
★ ★ ★ ★ ★ ★		30
★ ★ ★ ★ ★ ★		40
★ ★ ★ ★ ★ ★		50
★ ★ ★ ★ ★ ★		60

HOW TO PLAY
SLEUTH & SOLVE!

You can solve these mysteries with family and friends. The more people participate, the more fun the game will be! But even if you are playing with just one other person, you will still enjoy the game. You can even play alone and try to solve the puzzles on your own. Then you will become a real detective, looking for clues and using both logic and imagination. There are a few ways to play:

AS A FAMILY

• Make sure you set aside enough time to play. You don't want to be rushed.

• For maximum fun, have several detectives participate (the more players, the more fun)!

• One person should look at the solution under the flap before you begin solving the mystery—they will be the Investigation Director (you can change the director for each case). The other detectives will ask questions about the case in order to get clues. The director can only respond with the following types of answers:

  - With a "yes" or "no."

  - By posing a question (when it's clear that some clue hasn't been understood).

  - With "It doesn't matter" (when the question isn't relevant to finding the solution).

• If you get stuck, the Investigation Director can help you review the clues and observe anything that may have been overlooked.

To keep score, you can write down points on a sheet of paper or in a notebook.

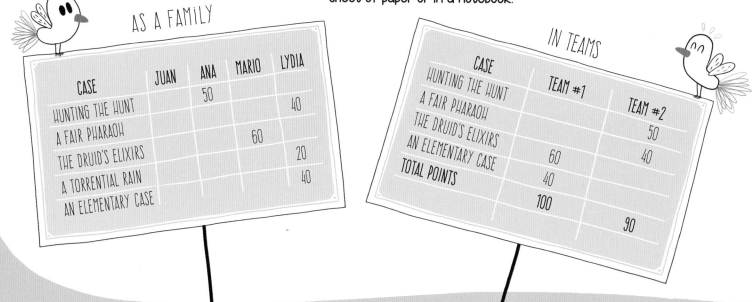

AS A FAMILY

CASE	JUAN	ANA	MARIO	LYDIA
HUNTING THE HUNT		50		40
A FAIR PHARAOH			60	
THE DRUID'S ELIXIRS				20
A TORRENTIAL RAIN				40
AN ELEMENTARY CASE				

IN TEAMS

CASE	TEAM #1	TEAM #2
HUNTING THE HUNT		
A FAIR PHARAOH		50
THE DRUID'S ELIXIRS	60	40
AN ELEMENTARY CASE	40	
TOTAL POINTS	100	90

IN TEAMS

REMEMBER, WE ALL THINK DIFFERENTLY! CASES THAT MAY SEEM EASY TO YOU MAY BE DIFFICULT FOR OTHER PEOPLE, AND THE OTHER WAY AROUND.

• Form teams of two or more detectives, and ask another person to be the judge.

• Before you begin investigating, determine the number of cases each team will solve. To win, you don't have to solve the cases faster than other teams—you just have to earn more points!

• When a team finds the solution, tell the judge. The judge will determine whether the team has earned the points and may continue on to the next case.

• Every time a team solves a case, the judge will write down the points earned on a piece of paper. If there is a tie between teams, solve another case to resolve the tie.

BY YOURSELF

• You can also solve these mysteries on your own and keep track of your points.

Elementary, my dear friends! It's time to start sleuthing and solving!

TABLE OF CONTENTS

Welcome!

PREHISTORIC TIMES: 200,000–4000 B.C.

Humanity has come a long way since *Homo sapiens* first appeared on Earth. By thinking, imagining, creating, and solving puzzles, human beings made huge strides toward establishing civilization.

PREHISTORIC TIMES

THE OLD AGES: 4000 B.C.–A.D. 476

The humans who shared the same territory and culture were grouped into great societies known as the first ancient civilizations. It was then that writing was invented, and the first cities and organized religions emerged. The Roman Empire spread everywhere.

THE MIDDLE AGES: A.D. 500–1400

The invasion of Germanic peoples in Europe disintegrated the Roman Empire and gave rise to a new map and European society. Land passed into the hands of feudal lords, who often exploited their vassals. It was a dark time, rife with epidemics and religious wars known as the Crusades. During this period, the Church influenced all aspects of people's lives. However, everything would soon change with the appearance of a new mode of inquiry known as the Renaissance.

THE MODERN ERA: A.D. 1400–1800

The quest for new sea trade routes led to the development of precise navigational instruments that guided European navigators to two continents: America and Oceania. A new value system prizing reason, communication, and innovative progress arose, and the invention of the printing press allowed the wide dissemination of these ideas. People now demanded equality and, as a result, several revolutions broke out, bringing with them the rise of citizens' individual rights.

THE CONTEMPORARY ERA: A.D. 1800–TODAY

The progress of humanity was directly linked to unstoppable human ingenuity. The invention of the steam engine enabled mass production of goods, and cities became industrialized as a result. One great invention followed another: the electric light, the telephone, the motorcar, and the airplane, to name a few. And although the twentieth century began with two lamentable World Wars, humanity increasingly turned its focus to improving communication: The press became globalized with the advent of television, radio, movies, and the most revolutionary medium of our time—the internet. Now, humanity is faced with one of our most exciting mysteries to date: life in space.

THE CONTEMPORARY ERA

PREHISTORIC TIMES
200,000–4000 B.C.

LOGIC

POINTS
10

LEVEL / VERY EASY
★ ☆ ☆ ☆ ☆ ☆

The Upper Paleolithic Era (Old Stone Age): 40,000–8000 B.C.
The two biggest priorities of Stone Age societies were finding food and keeping peace among a group's inhabitants.

STONE AGE SUSPICIONS

In this particular Stone Age tribe, one of the most serious crimes was stealing food. The punishment for such a terrible crime was banishment. And since it was very difficult to survive without the help of a community, this was the worst punishment of all.

Every day, the tribe's hunters ventured out while everyone else remained near the cave. There was so much work to be done, such as preparing a bonfire to roast the previous day's catch for the next few days. But one morning, when preparing the meat for the fire . . .

1 A woman sounded the alarm:

Someone has stolen the meat!

2 The group's members were enraged and consulted their wisest elder to help them find the culprit.

3 A child approached the elder and whispered something in his ear:

I saw the man with a "face of fire" take the meat.

I know who did it!

4 The elder reflected on these strange words and then looked closely at everyone gathered around the bonfire.

WHO STOLE THE MEAT? ?

13

PREHISTORIC TIMES
200,000–4000 B.C.

IMAGINATION

POINTS
50

LEVEL / DIFFICULT
★ ★ ★ ★ ★ ✦

The Mesolithic Era: 8000-2700 B.C.

After the Ice Age, the climate improved and some animals began to migrate north. Humans were still nomadic, but stayed in one place longer than most species. They still depended on large animals for food, warm clothes, and survival. Every year, before the cold arrived, humans had to search for food that they could store and eat during the long winter.

HUNTING THE HUNT

The hunter of this tribe sharpened his weapon and stone tools, then set off to hunt the large animals that would keep the group fed throughout the winter. But first, he had to figure out where to find them . . .

1 Several days into his long journey, the hunter stumbled upon a shaman.

2 The shaman consulted nature spirits by performing an ancestral rite, asking them where the hunter should travel in order to find food.

3 Entering a deep trance, the shaman said:

To the north lies the great river. Cross it after two full moons. On the other side, you will find the animals you are seeking.

4 The hunter could not swim, but when he came to the great river, he waited for two full moons and then crossed it without drowning.

And indeed, the other shore was teeming with large animals!

wow!

HOW DID THE HUNTER GET ACROSS THE RIVER?

15

THE OLD AGES
4000 B.C.–A.D.476

IMAGINATION

POINTS
50

LEVEL / DIFFICULT
★★★★★☆

The Babylonian Empire: 2300-539 B.C.

The Babylonian Empire was established on the Euphrates River in ancient Mesopotamia. Under King Hammurabi's rule, Babylon became one of the biggest cities in the ancient world. In addition to overseeing the rise of the military, Hammurabi was credited with creating one of the most extensive legal codes, known as the Code of Hammurabi.

ELUDING THE LAW

The Babylonian Empire's citizens had to pay the king a portion of the proceeds from their business transactions, especially when it came to pack animals and grains, which were considered luxury goods. On one occasion, the guards of the great gate of Babylon became suspicious of a man who entered the city each day with a mule loaded with stones, and then left the city every day with a bag full of money, as if he'd conducted business . . .

16

1 Every morning, Nabu entered the city with a young, strong mule, whose packs were loaded with two sacks full of stones.

2 When the soldiers ordered him to show his merchandise every morning, Nabu opened the sacks and they let him pass, since there were no taxes on stones.

Go ahead, you may pass.

3 Every afternoon, Nabu left the city with a slow and tired mule, but an overflowing bag of money.

Huff, Huff

4 The guards were suspicious because they suspected that Nabu was cheating the tax . . . until they discovered what he was selling.

WHAT WAS NABU SELLING? ?

17

the old ages
4000 B.C.–A.D. 476

IMAGINATION

POINTS
40

LEVEL / MEDIUM
★ ★ ★ ★ ★ ★

Ancient Egypt: 3100–30 B.C.

The Ancient Egyptian civilization was led for millennia by families who succeeded each other in dynasties. The ruler of each dynasty was known as a pharaoh and considered a god. Pharaohs were almost always male, with some exceptions. There was Queen Hatshepsut, who improved the economy and brought peace to Egypt, although she had to dress like a man to be accepted as a pharaoh!

A FAIR PHARAOH

The Egyptian line of succession was not always simple, especially if the pharaoh had no children and there was no queen to succeed him upon his death. This was true in the case of one pharaoh, who chose his successor using a very ingenious method . . .

1. The pharaoh wanted to determine who would be an honest successor, so he devised a clever test: He ordered that a pot filled with earth be distributed to every child in Egypt. After one year, each child would return their pot to the palace.

ONE YEAR LATER...

2. The children were summoned to the palace with their pots. Some of the pots were now filled with beautiful flowers, while others were filled with plants of every shape and size.

3. Only one girl returned the pot without any plant in it at all, exactly as it had been given to her. Upon seeing this, the pharaoh acted immediately.

I have made my decision. You will be my successor.

Thank you! I will try to be a great pharaoh.

WHY DID THE PHARAOH CHOOSE THE CHILD WHO HAD *NOT* BROUGHT HIM A PLANT?

?

THE OLD AGES
4000 B.C.–A.D. 476

IMAGINATION

POINTS
30

LEVEL / MEDIUM
★★★☆☆☆

The Ancient Greeks: 800-146 B.C.

The Ancient Greeks lived in the Mediterranean region near the Aegean Sea. They were expert sailors and merchants, and they founded vast cities such as Athens and Sparta. Ancient Greek ideas continue to influence modern society, impacting art, math, science, theories of government, and even the evolution of democracy.

THE MOST INTELLIGENT PERSON

Pericles was one of the most prominent Athenian statesmen, and he liked to surround himself with artists and thinkers. His partner was Aspasia de Mileto, a cultured woman and the subject of many tales, not all of them true. This is one such anecdote, in which Pericles issued a challenge to the Athenians . . .

1 Pericles announced:

He who covers me with this tunic from head to toe will be named the smartest man in Athens.

2 Several men tried, but none could cover Pericles completely.

GRRR!

?

3 Aspasia, annoyed that only men had been invited to participate in the challenge, offered to solve the puzzle.

I know how to do it.

4 Aspasia asked Pericles to do two things. The first was to lie on the tunic, which she placed on the floor. Then she asked him to do a second thing which would allow her to cover him with the tunic completely.

5 And she solved the puzzle! Pericles had the title of the award amended to the most intelligent *person* in Athens.

You are the best!   I know.

WHAT WAS THE SECOND THING ASPASIA TOLD PERICLES TO DO?

?

THE OLD AGES
4000 B.C.–A.D. 476

LOGIC

POINTS
60

LEVEL / VERY DIFFICULT
★ ★ ★ ★ ★ ★

The Celts: 1200-450 B.C.

The need for weapons and utensils led humans to the discovery of metals. Copper, bronze, and iron not only facilitated more efficient farming, but helped when it came to defending against other tribes. During the Iron Age, the Celts were known as fierce and brave warriors–a reputation they earned from the concoctions prepared by their priests who were known as druids.

THE DRUID'S ELIXIRS

Before a battle, it was a Celtic druid tradition to gather the men and women who would lead the attack. Sometimes they prepared concoctions to make these leaders invincible. But not everyone liked the same herbs . . .

1 A druid was preparing five different potions, using a different herb for each one: juniper berries, St. John's wort, verbena, peppermint, and sage.

23

2 He had heard that battle-hardened Ydris loved verbena.

I love verbena.

3 Brian and Erin liked St. John's wort, although Erin used to enjoy juniper berry infusions.

4 Maere hated juniper berries and *detested* mint.

5 Since he knew that Brian and Neil liked juniper berries, the druid was able to quickly figure out who would get each potion.

GIVEN EACH OF THEIR PREFERENCES, WHICH WARRIOR GOT A POTION MADE OUT OF WHICH HERB?

Draw a line from each potion to the warrior who drank it.

| JUNIPER BERRIES | ST. JOHN'S WORT | VERBENA | PEPPERMINT | SAGE |

| YDRIS | BRIAN | ERIN | MAERE | NEIL |

FOR WHOM DID THE DRUID PREPARE EACH POTION?

25

THE OLD AGES
4000 B.C.–A.D. 476

LOGIC

POINTS
50

LEVEL / DIFFICULT
★ ★ ★ ★ ★ ☆

The Roman Civilization under Caligula: A.D. 37-41

The Roman Empire eventually spread from the Mediterranean to lands as distant as the United Kingdom and even to certain areas of Africa. For five centuries, the Romans imposed their laws, language, and way of life upon the regions they conquered. And several of their emperors would be known for their follies, too.

THE EMPEROR'S PLAN

Some say that the third Roman emperor, Caligula, adored his horse, Incitatus, so much that he had an ivory manger constructed in its honor. And it was said that Caligula even wanted to appoint Incitatus a Roman senator! So when a good citizen was unfairly accused of trying to steal his beloved horse, Caligula was on the case . . .

1. The emperor knew that the jury would declare the accused man innocent because he was an exemplary citizen.

2. In order to avoid accusations of being unfair, the emperor proclaimed:

Let the gods judge him!

He he

3. The emperor then put two papers into a bowl. One read GUILTY, and the other *should* have read INNOCENT . . . but Caligula wrote GUILTY on that one, too.

Gulp!

4. However, the accused man saw Caligula's trick. After choosing one of the papers from the bowl, he swallowed it instead of showing it to the jury! The jury then declared him innocent.

WHY DID THE JURY DECLARE THE MAN INNOCENT?

?

THE OLD AGES
4000 B.C.–A.D. 476

LOGIC

POINTS
50

LEVEL / DIFFICULT
★★★★★☆

Ancient Scientists: Archimedes: 287 B.C.

In ancient times, reason and logic were used to explain everything, like the universe and existence. One of the most popular scientists was Archimedes of Syracuse, who is credited with discovering the center of gravity, and other important laws of physics. During a siege of his city, Archimedes also invented ingenious weapons, including concave mirrors that were used to burn enemy ships.

THE WEIGHT OF THE CROWN

On one occasion, King Hiero of Syracuse asked Archimedes how to know if a goldsmith was cheating him. The king had given a gold ingot to a certain goldsmith so that it could be made into a crown. However, the king feared that the goldsmith had only used part of the gold, keeping the rest for himself. Were his fears correct?

1 After hearing the king's concerns, Archimedes returned to his house and prepared a bath while deep in thought. When he got into the bathtub, he noticed that the water rose up to the edge of the tub, even though it had been lower before he got in.

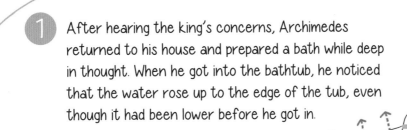

EUREKA!
I know how to find out!

2 Suddenly, Archimedes was struck with a great realization: He knew how to check whether the goldsmith had cheated the king! Archimedes ran back to the palace as fast as he could, still dripping wet and barely clothed.

3 At the palace, Archimedes asked for two containers of water. He put the crown in one container and a gold ingot in the other. The level of water in the ingot's container rose much higher than the level of water in the crown's container!

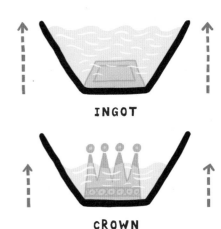

INGOT

CROWN

This goldsmith has cheated me!

4 Upon seeing the result of the experiment, the king accused the goldsmith of stealing.

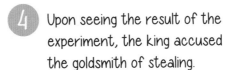

HOW DID THE KING KNOW THAT THE ENTIRE INGOT HADN'T BEEN USED?

THE MIDDLE AGES
A.D. 500–1400

LOGIC

POINTS
50

LEVEL / DIFFICULT
★ ★ ★ ★ ★ ☆

The Barbarian Invasions: A.D. 300–700

During the first centuries of the Common Era, a wave of Germanic people migrated south due to the cold and lack of crops. Because they lived outside the Roman Empire's borders, they were called *barbari,* which means "foreigners" in Latin. Their looting plunged Europe into chaos and the Roman Empire disappeared shortly after.

FOLLOW ME!
TO ROME!

BEWARE OF THE BARBARIANS

Alaric, the Visigoth king, had crossed into Italy with his warriors, so the Romans sent spies to learn the details of their advance. When the spies found out that the barbarians intended to attack and loot Rome, they galloped back to warn of the imminent invasion . . .

1 When the first spy arrived back at the gates of Rome, he had to say a password to be let inside. From inside, the guard yelled, "ONE!" The spy yelled back, "THREE!" Immediately, the gate was opened.

2 Shortly after, the next sweaty spy came galloping back to the gates of Rome. From inside, the guard shouted, "THREE!" And the soldier answered, "FIVE!" Again, the gate was opened.

3 With the stress of knowing that the Visigoths were hot on their heels, the last spy forgot the password! Instead, he tried to deduce it from the answers of his companions.

4 From inside, the guard shouted, "FIVE!" And the spy answered, "SEVEN!" But the gates didn't open.

WHAT NUMBER SHOULD THE SPY HAVE SAID?

THE MIDDLE AGES
A.D. 500–1400

LOGIC

POINTS
10

LEVEL / VERY EASY
★ ☆ ☆ ☆ ☆ ☆

Gentlemen, Nobles, Vassals, and Heroes: A.D. 1300

Under the feudal system of the Middle Ages, lords owned vast expanses of land and demanded tribute from the people, known as vassals, who lived there. This system created a great sense of inequality and injustice. Over time, literature turned some of this period's heroes into iconic characters, such as Robin Hood, who robbed the rich to help those in need.

ROBIN HOOD'S LESSON

Robin Hood trained his band of outcasts in the woods of England's Sherwood Forest. One day, he devised a clever test to make sure that everyone knew how to orient themselves within the forest in case they ever got lost.

① Robin determined the starting positions.

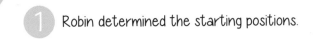

First, everyone start by facing West!

② Now, Will, turn 90° to the right!

③ Friar Tuck, turn 180° to the right!

④ Little John, turn 90° to the left!

⑤ Much, turn 180° to the left!

In which direction does each person's face now point? Use the compass below to orient yourself and find out.

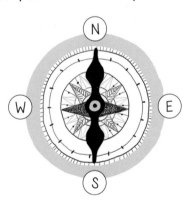

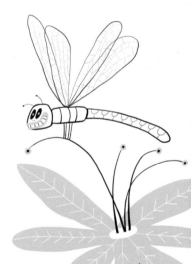

IN WHICH DIRECTION DOES EACH PERSON'S ARROW POINT?

THE MODERN ERA
A.D. 1400–1800

LOGIC

POINTS
10

LEVEL / VERY EASY
★ ★ ★ ★ ★

Renaissance Artists: A.D. 1500

In the fifteenth century, cultural ideals experienced a great shift, and emphasis was placed on reason, beauty, and classical thought. From this ideology the Italian Renaissance was born. The Renaissance was a cultural movement that produced great artists such as Leonardo da Vinci, who designed flying machines and developed the skill of mirror writing so that nobody would copy his ideas.

THE MYSTERY OF THE
MONA LISA

It so happened that Leonardo was commissioned to paint the portrait of a woman, but his client demanded that the artist could never reveal her identity. Leonardo had good reason to keep the identity a secret since his client was a powerful man and the subject was a married woman. (Some say she was married to Francesco del Giocondo, which is why the painting is also sometimes called "La Gioconda.")

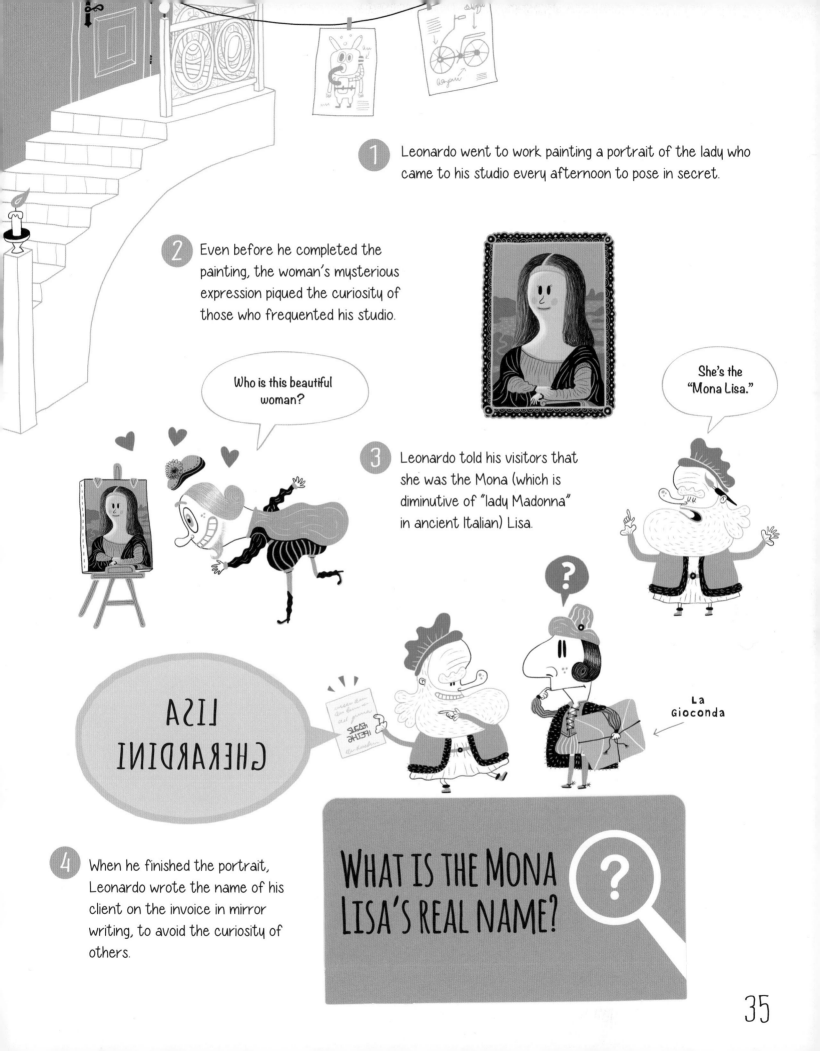

1 Leonardo went to work painting a portrait of the lady who came to his studio every afternoon to pose in secret.

2 Even before he completed the painting, the woman's mysterious expression piqued the curiosity of those who frequented his studio.

Who is this beautiful woman?

She's the "Mona Lisa."

3 Leonardo told his visitors that she was the Mona (which is diminutive of "lady Madonna" in ancient Italian) Lisa.

LISA GHERARDINI

La Gioconda

4 When he finished the portrait, Leonardo wrote the name of his client on the invoice in mirror writing, to avoid the curiosity of others.

WHAT IS THE MONA LISA'S REAL NAME? ?

THE MODERN ERA
A.D. 1400–1800

IMAGINATION

POINTS
40

LEVEL / MEDIUM
★ ★ ★ ★ ★ ★

Europeans Arrive in America: A.D. 1500

Christopher Columbus was a sailor who, in addition to being a good navigator, insisted on following a route that no other European settlers had traveled. In 1492, he landed on islands in the Carribean, changing the course of history with his journey.

COLUMBUS'S CHALLENGE

It is said that, upon returning to Europe from this distant land, Columbus was invited to many parties. He was not fond of these gatherings, however, because some tried to belittle his travels.

1. One night, Columbus attended a large banquet thrown by noble gentlemen. At the reception, one of them commented:

> If *you* hadn't traveled to the Indies, one of this country's *other* great navigators would have done it instead.

2. Columbus, annoyed by the comment, asked a servant to bring him an egg.

3. Columbus put the egg on the table and then posed a challenge:

> Since there are many talented people here tonight, I am sure one of you can make this egg stand up on the table without any help.

4. Many tried to balance the egg, without success. Finally, Columbus stepped in and, with a quick gesture, had the egg standing straight up on its own!

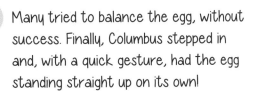

voilà!

HOW DID COLUMBUS GET THE EGG TO STAND?

THE MODERN ERA
A.D. 1400–1800

IMAGINATION

POINTS
40

LEVEL / MEDIUM
★ ★ ★ ★ ☆

The Aztec Empire: A.D. 1428-1521

When Spanish conquerors came to South America, they communicated with the Mayan people through an interpreter known as Malinche. She served as the conquistador Hernán Cortés's confidante, and explained many Mayan and Aztec customs to the Spaniards, such as drinking the cacao concoction, *xocoatl.*

A CURIOUS CONCOCTION

Cortés was invited by the Aztec king Montezuma II to taste a glass full of a dark and cold liquid. He was wary at first, but Malinche explained that it was made from chocolate, which is prepared by grinding cacao beans into powder, then adding water. Back then, the cacao fruit was so valuable that its seeds were used as currency!

1 A few minutes earlier, a chef in the Tenochtitlán palace kitchen ground cacao beans to prepare chocolate for the visitors.

2 One of the king's warriors watched intently to make sure that Montezuma and his guests would not be poisoned.

3 Suddenly, the chef turned around and tripped over the warrior, spilling some of the bowl's contents on him.

Ah!

?

4 However, the warrior's clothes stayed dry!

WHY DIDN'T THE WARRIOR'S CLOTHES GET WET? ❓

THE MODERN ERA
A.D. 1400–1800

IMAGINATION

POINTS
20

LEVEL / EASY
★ ★ ☆ ☆ ☆ ☆ ☆

European Fashion: sixteenth-seventeenth century A.D.

The umbrella was invented in China long before it became fashionable to Italian and French aristocrats in the seventeenth century. People used umbrellas in both the sun and rain, and the folding umbrella became widely used throughout Europe after its introduction–except in England, where it was considered a woman's accessory.

A TORRENTIAL RAIN

Jonas Hanway was an English businessman who returned from one of his trips with something that Londoners in the 1750s considered unusual: an umbrella. Every time he went walking with it, everyone made fun of him. Some carriage drivers even tried to attack him because the invention of the umbrella threatened their business! (The rain was a boon for carriage drivers.)

1. One afternoon, Jonas was walking through the streets of London to his favorite restaurant with an umbrella in tow. He was accompanied by his business colleagues, Taylor and Clark.

2. As they were walking, it began to pour. Jonas opened his umbrella while his companions ran toward the restaurant to get out of the rain.

JONAS   TAYLOR   CLARK

3. When Taylor arrived at the restaurant, his hair was soaking wet.

4. But Clark's hair didn't get wet at all, even though he had no hat or umbrella, and he hadn't taken shelter anywhere, either.

HOW IS THIS POSSIBLE?

THE MODERN ERA
A.D. 1400–1800

LOGIC

POINTS
60

LEVEL / VERY DIFFICULT
★ ★ ★ ★ ★ ★

The French Revolution: A.D. 1789

Tired of going hungry while kings and nobles lived in luxury, the French people revolted. Crowds took to the streets, assaulted the palace, and beheaded the nobles while crying, "To the guillotine!" and proclaiming, "Freedom, equality, and brotherhood." The French Revolution paved the way for the people to participate in government, but it terrified the nobility.

TO CATCH A
JEWEL THIEF

The French royals were waiting for the right moment to flee Paris with the help of the queen's friend, Swedish marshal Axel von Fersen. Accompanying the royal party was an ambitious and wealthy count. A day before the planned escape, the count summoned the chief of police regarding the disappearance of a large diamond. The count accused Queen Marie Antoinette of stealing it.

1. The count explained his version of events to the chief of police:

"It was a dark and moonless night. A noise woke me up, and I looked out the window without turning on the lights in case the revolutionaries came to cut off our heads."

2. He described the events in great detail:

"It was raining outside, but I could see the shadow of Axel von Fersen cast on the opposite wall with his unmistakable three-cornered hat."

3. "When I went down to the first floor of the palace, the royal treasure chamber was open."

4. Then the count insinuated that the queen was behind the theft:

"It was then that I discovered the diamond had been stolen and I sounded the alarm. Everyone knows that von Fersen needs money—and the queen gives him anything he asks for."

5. But the chief of police chastised the count instead:

Sir, return the diamond. It's obvious who is really lying.

HOW DID THE CHIEF OF POLICE KNOW THAT THE COUNT WAS THE THIEF?

THE MODERN ERA
A.D. 1400–1800

LOGIC

POINTS
20

LEVEL / EASY
★ ★ ☆ ☆ ☆ ☆ ☆

Napoleon the Great: A.D. 1799-1815

After the upheaval of the French Revolution, General Napoleon Bonaparte tried to impose a new order in France and across Europe, which he invaded with his large army. He crowned himself emperor in 1804, and then defeated the Austrians and Russians in the Battle of Austerlitz one year later.

DO YOU UNDERSTAND?

Two soldiers of the French army were each charged with watching an end of the bridge near Austerlitz, to keep the Austrians and Russians from attacking the French camp. But would they be able to carry out their orders?

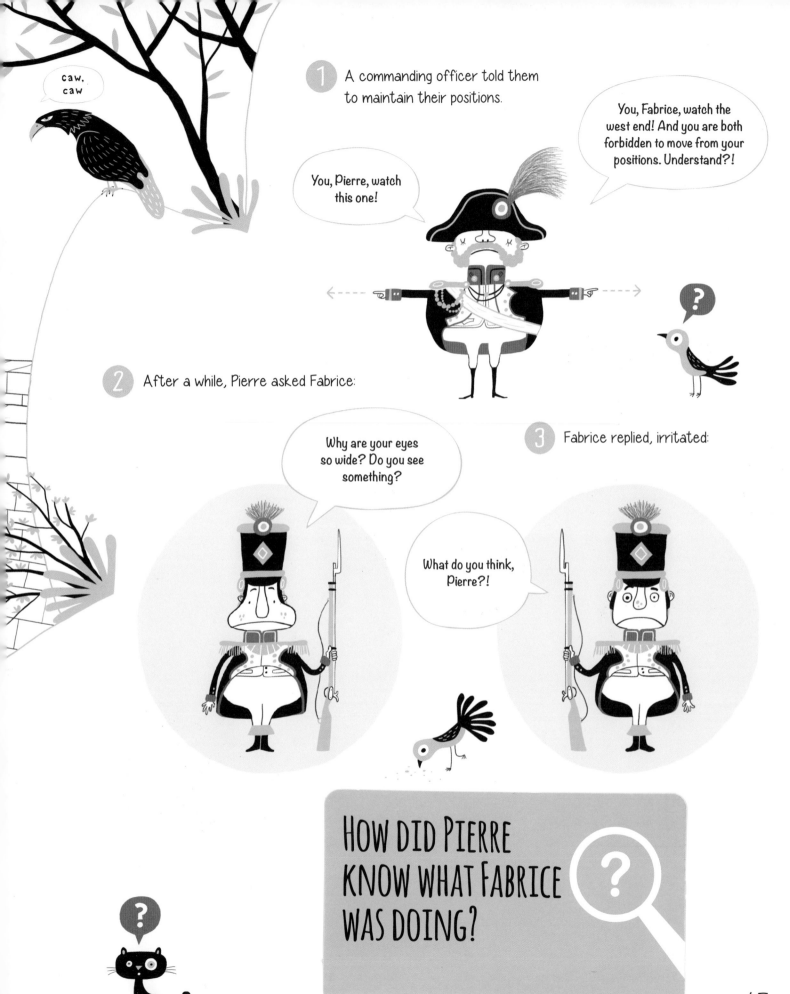

THE CONTEMPORARY ERA
A.D. 1800–Today

IMAGINATION

POINTS
60

LEVEL / VERY DIFFICULT
★ ★ ★ ★ ★ ★

A Great Inventor: Thomas Edison, nineteenth century A.D.

Some of the most important inventions of the nineteenth century were made by Thomas Edison and his contemporaries. Hundreds of inventions came out of the Edison laboratory, including the motion picture camera to record movies, the phonograph to record music, and a battery for electric cars.

A BRIGHT IDEA

Many stories of uncertain origin and validity have been told about Edison, and one of them is this: Edison's grandfather wanted to leave his inheritance to one of his three grandchildren, but he didn't know which one to choose. To test them, he gave each grandchild some money and told them to buy something that could completely fill the family barn.

1. The eldest bought two wagons full of wood. But, once unloaded, they did not fill the barn.

2. The middle grandchild bought two wagons full of straw, but they did not fill the barn, either.

3. The youngest, Thomas Edison, had a bright idea: He only bought two objects, and yet he managed to completely fill the barn by using them.

4. Not only did Edison save almost all of the money from his grandfather, he was the one who received his grandfather's fortune.

I'm leaving!

WHAT DID YOUNG EDISON USE TO FILL THE BARN?

THE CONTEMPORARY ERA
A.D. 1800–Today

LOGIC

POINTS
40

LEVEL / MEDIUM
★ ★ ★ ★ ★ ★

A Unique Detective: Sherlock Holmes, nineteenth-twentieth century A.D.

Sherlock Holmes is so famous that many people believe he really existed. Alas, this detective was a fictional creation of the English writer Sir Arthur Conan Doyle. Holmes was a somewhat eccentric investigator whose superior reasoning skills allowed him   to solve even the most complicated crimes–although, for him, everything that could be deduced with logic was simply "elementary."

AN ELEMENTARY CASE

Sherlock Holmes was returning from his walk in Regent's Park when he saw some people gathered around a body on the ground. The detective approached, and immediately discovered that the poor chap was dead. After examining his pockets, Holmes found the man's driver's license, which contained his personal information.

1 Holmes learned that the man's name was Lord Richard Adams. Not far from the body, he found a place to call the deceased man's home phone.

2 Mrs. Adams answered the phone. The detective informed her that her husband's body had been found. Stunned, Mrs. Adams quickly hung up the phone.

My goodness! I'll be there right away.

Mrs. Adams, we need you to identify the body. Can you come as soon as possible?

3 Several minutes later, Mrs. Adams arrived and, upon seeing her deceased husband, began to cry.

BOO HOO! BOO HOO!!

4 Holmes thought for a moment, then told the police:

Arrest this woman! She is the murderer.

HOW DID HOLMES KNOW?

THE CONTEMPORARY ERA
A.D. 1800–Today

IMAGINATION

POINTS
40

LEVEL / MEDIUM
★ ★ ★ ★ ★ ☆ ☆

The Daily Newspaper: nineteenth century A.D.

The great revolution of the press occurred at the beginning of the nineteenth century. Thanks to the telegraph and the telephone, events from around the world could be relayed quickly and then printed in newspapers. People eagerly awaited the news to the point that newspapers became a product as essential to daily life as bread or milk.

A FREE SERVICE

Don was an older gentleman who shared a nice apartment with his best friend, Bruno. Don's only habit was reading the newspaper every morning while enjoying his breakfast. But since they didn't get the paper delivered to their house, Bruno was in charge of picking it up every day.

1 Every morning while Don was having breakfast, Bruno would run to the nearby newsstand in search of the day's newspaper.

2 In less than five minutes, Bruno returned with the newspaper and rang the doorbell to be let back in the apartment.

3 Don opened the door and Bruno gave him the newspaper.

DING!

DONG!

4 Every day for many years, Bruno never failed Don, not even once. He even went to get the newspaper on weekends! But Don never offered to pay him for this generous service.

WHY DIDN'T DON PAY BRUNO FOR HIS HELP?

THE CONTEMPORARY ERA
A.D. 1800–TODAY

LOGIC

POINTS
50

LEVEL / DIFFICULT
★ ★ ★ ★ ★ ★ ★

The Greatest Magician: Houdini, twentieth century A.D.

In the early twentieth century, the great magician Harry Houdini took the intimate magic of street fairs and turned it into a spectacular, full-theater show. He could free himself from chains and padlocks, escape from a straitjacket, and untie himself while underwater.

A MAGICIAN'S MYSTERY

This is one of the many legends recounted about his powers: The owner of the theater where Houdini was scheduled to perform decided to give him an impossibly difficult test that would draw more crowds than ever before. Houdini would not be chained like he had been in the past. Rather, he would be placed in a room—a room where he could die if left inside!

1 Houdini was taken into a room with two mysterious doors.

2 The first door opened onto a room made from magnifying glass. The sun shone through the walls, fatally burning anyone who tried to cross it.

3 Behind the second door was a hungry beast, impatiently waiting for his food.

ROOOOOOOAAAAAR!

4 But, to everyone's amazement, Houdini managed to leave the room safe and sound.

WHICH DOOR DID HOUDINI USE TO LEAVE?

THE CONTEMPORARY ERA
A.D. 1800–Today

LOGIC

POINTS
30

LEVEL / MEDIUM
★ ★ ★ ★ ★ ★

World War II: A.D. 1939-1945

During World War II, the Germans communicated using encrypted messages thanks to their invention of the Enigma machine. However, Polish cryptographers managed to crack their codes and successfully avoided many attacks by the Nazi army.

What should I spy on today?

A SHOCKING REVEAL

Marek was a cryptographer for the resistance fighting against the Nazis. He was collaborating with Ania Anders, the daughter of Jan Anders, a Polish businessman. Ania was in charge of monitoring the movements of those who were suspected of helping the Nazis. To communicate the names of suspects with Ania in secret, the cryptographer taught her a simple code.

1 This is how the secret code worked:

Then, change each letter of the encrypted message to the letter above or below it. Look, here's how you would write "Marek:"

Z N E R X

First, divide the alphabet into two rows: from A to M and from N to Z.

A B C D E F G H I J K L M
N O P Q R S T U V W X Y Z

2 Ania was very good at watching the suspects because she knew many people. And, thanks to her father's reputation, nobody suspected her.

3 One morning, Ania went to pick up the coded message from Marek in the usual place.

4 When she deciphered it, Ania turned pale and exclaimed:

WNA NAQREF

Oh, no! I can't believe it!

WHY WAS ANIA UPSET?

?

THE CONTEMPORARY ERA
A.D. 1800–Today

LOGIC

POINTS
40

LEVEL / MEDIUM
★★★★★★★

The Space Age: twentieth–twenty-first century A.D.

Since the 1980s, the technology revolution has changed the world. The information superhighway has connected everyone, allowing people to exchange information and connect with each other immediately and directly. And, thanks to technology, we are embarking on one of the most exciting adventures yet: space travel!

THE PASSWORD

On a space station, both ground operators and astronauts have a personal password to access their computers. If a password is entered incorrectly three times, the computer is locked and a new password is automatically created. And that's just what happened to the astronaut Celeste one morning . . .